Don't underestimate my emotions for you.....

as they flow deeper than my rivers.....

calm as the waters.....

but strong as the ocean......

I can see what I hear.....

and taste what I feel….

so please.....

don't underestimate my emotions....

for you.....deep rivers

He is my master

As I am his student....protégé

Yes I am his masterpiece

With every command. ...my body reacts

The soft stern voice.

Exhilarating chills that skip rope up and down my spine

Yes I am his student....submissive

Every minute I smile is the result of the pleasure I receive

in pleasing him

Seeing the satisfaction in his eyes

The eye of my soul

Burns for the respect and love that he gives me

I inhale to exhale to taste his scent

To bask in the illumination of his shining armor

Yes he is my knight.......my love

My everything.....

Published by Amorous Ink Publishing
Indianapolis, IN 46205

ISBN 9781943159130

LCCN 2018953074

The publisher would appreciate notification where errors occur so that they may be corrected in subsequent printing and/or

Slip of the Tongue

By

Deep Rivers

Love me as I love you more......taste my tears....as they flow with the flavor of sweet wine.....caress my skin....as you are the warmth that heats my everything....just a simple passing thought of you....and blazing flames reach from below.....to the atmosphere of my heart.....I close my eyes and see you so clearly.....waiting for that moment when I lay my hands upon your beating heart.....trapped beneath what was.....stripping the layers of hard strength.....in search of a heart. ....that is pure....loving and protective.....of what you love.....so far away....but yet so near. ....you and I have yet to meet....but my soul already knows....that it's soul mate.....awaits.....as my lips whisper.....I Love you.....know matter how far.....my words land upon yours…..

My soul is not your playground....and my spirit is not meant to be broken.....with the atrocities that you insist on draping me in....my heart has been mutilated....extracted.....and replaced with a mechanical repetitious.....on off switch…..the warmth...cold....dark and stripped....my love....captured....held hostage.....as what remains. ..needs to be rejuvenated. ..with hope and faith.....as my mind shattered into pieces of the words....that are needed to start again.....a heart the size of the universe. ...treated like outdated memories ...with no change in sight....my soul is not your playground.....grown folks play in the real world.....not fairy tell land......I'm done.....running on empty......so I'm going nowhere fast....Love has cost me everything....my reward. ...nothing....deep rivers

My heart dances to the darkness

which allows the soul its freedom

flying free to a blank canvas

Kiss me until I say stop

Pampered by each kiss you give

no need to rush the moment

the beauty in taking it slow

If he only knew the truth

truth that releases both of us

Trust starts within then with others

Very true from start to finish

And everyone believes in their truth

Many die that should never die

While others live that should die

Never underestimate my complex creative mind

Truth the sincerity of my depth

A force that soothes with words

Closed eyes that see with clarity

while ears hear what's not said

Understand before you try to advise

The book more than a cover

Understand my words and their story….

Mental Playground

You have not a clue

This is not what you think

This is pass all normal understanding

This is not for the mild, meek or sensitive

It is just that a mental playground

My mental playground

My words draw you in and the need to know more

To explore

To see how real

Not knowing if it is

My mental playground

My reality is beyond most fantasies

I am who I am

That I do not apologize for

I relish in who I am

My tongue uses your dick as my merry go round

My hands stroke you fast then slow

Just like a child in a swing

Push me higher

The power to make you do just as I please

And at times I never say a word

You know or you will be dismissed

And that you definitely don't want me to do

I command you to be very still as I straddle you

I spin, slow grind and manipulate your body to my pleasure

Beyond your wildest dreams

As you beg to release

Pussy massages all of you and you moan and groan

And I forbid you to move

My mental playground

As I fuck you long and hard

Wet and wild

My rivers flow and you still beg to release

And at that very moment I remove myself

And allow you to jack off

My playground my rules…..

Oralipstic Talents

When my past.....releases pieces of what....will be.....should decide.....that deep desire.....lust that battles with love.....to taste the significance.....while seducing what no longer sees.......boundaries of flesh.....pinned beneath....flashes of light.....as his tongue strips what control....my mind thought it had.....body betrayed.....orgasms scream...,,and flows fluently across his lips.....as I fight to contained.....but the pleasure....demands more....And all hell breaks loose......as my past releases more pieces of my present....only to await the future....as his tongue drained my soul......deep rivers

As I sip on the warmth of my hot white chocolate mocha

With a scent that brings back the heat with much flava

I drift back to memories that you embedded deep in my
past, present and future

His eyes spoke to me from the top of my head

To the tips of my toes

That release when he allows me to

See…..

The torture performed is more than a masterpiece

It is the very descriptive being of all of me

He sculpts my lips by the kiss he gives

Gives direction to the heaving of my chest with the caress
of his hands

My thighs seem to swell with the journey that his tongue
ventures on

As my pleas get stronger

To release

And his whispers stay the same

Not yet

Allow me to please you from 1 to

No the numbers don't go that high

So let's just continue

When you really want it to be over

Push me away

And at that point my mind went into overload

I would die before I pushed him away

Or play tug of war with his body

Needing him next to mind

I need him to lick

Then suck my clit in circles

Telling me the time

As each lick, represents each hour on the clock

Clock of my sanity that no longer exists

I need his hands to squeeze my nipples just right

Or maybe a little harder to make my body flinch

With a dip of pleasure and a whip of pain

All awhile his dick is stroking me with a rhythm that has
taken me around the world and back

And I am not unpacking because I am ready to go again

And the finale

Is demonstrated with just the right

Touch

Pressure so delicately applied

As his grip around my neck

Held like precious pearls

And the rivers overflow with pleasure

And the orgasms keep going and going and going

Damn is this what the energizer bunny feels like

And if so let it flow

Over and over and over

And yes this is just the beginning

My desires need to be fed

I need him to give me…..

I want his tongue....to drink of my nectar.....while his hands play a melody. ....of African drums...bass guitar....and a violin solo.....with my breasts...,...that stand at attention with every note......submissive to his demands......waiting for that which takes me higher.....allowing my orgasms....to....float down continuously......as i will give him all that he desires…on command...,.he is me as I am him.......we have become one.....deep rivers

Slip your tongue in my hidden treasures

Straddle my canvas with artistry of your pleasure

When we meet in the middle of leather and lace

While latex wraps

With stiletto pumps crave and desire

You speak in a rhythm that never ceases

Creating a masterpiece of love and lust

A love that I crave

With lust that turns into my addiction

Power with only a whisper

And a whisper that screams desire

Chocolate steel that delivers stroke after stroke

Determined to break the dam and allow the rivers to flow

The beating of two hearts in sync

The aroma that has filled the room

As you have licked my reality

Sucked my dreams

And fucked me into totality

Hands placed just right with pressure so gently applied

And the light flashed in a dark room

At that moment I realize

That I want more…..of him…..

The taste

The flavor

The aroma

The scent

The reality that all of him has possessed all of me

He enters deep and pounds away all the tears that I can

imagine

And then he tells me that

He is just getting starting

He strokes over the moon into a meadow that is lost

nowhere

And somewhere in my mind

I don't want to be found

Stripped of any sensibility

All of my sensuality

Left

He grabbed my last bit of respect and sat it on the shelf to

watch

Spoke very clear and said if you want to leave you can

If you don't, you never will be the same again

I stayed

My legs took a quick class in gymnastics

As the rest of my body was bent lent and spent in so many

ways

Ways that I can't find definitions for

He licked and I moaned

He sucked and I screamed not to stop but for more

He fucked me in so many different ways

That between positions

Languages that were spoken

And the amount of fluids that flowed and drained

Only to be replenished

And drained again and again

My breathing left

And returned for the second and third shift

I lost track of the numerous orgasms

That he gave me

He licked, sucked and fucked me in ways that I could never

reveal

And that's because

I am now addicted to all of him

Share I will not

I need his tongue to continue to grace my dreams

And his dick to direct my reality

Nothing less will do

My desires have instructions attached

With demands that will be met

With the rising of the sun

And the falling of the rain

He gives me…

As my thoughts battle with reality

I slowly remove the blinders from the emotions

That don't stand a chance

See what I want

What he wants

Never seems to be what we want

At the same time

My mind cascades over the window of opportunity

And back to what makes me crave him

Lips that taste like fresh sliced mango

With a flavor sweeter than fresh honey

See what I want

What he wants

Never seems to be what we want

At the same time

I have an appetite

A craving that never ceases

I want to lick and suck him at will

Swallowing the whole length of him

Just because

I love how he screams my name when I do

I love to mount him and ride him slowly

No need to rush

If so

Please find your own way out

I feel his hands reach for me

One hand on my breast

While the other wraps itself

And waits

When I feel all beats speeding up

The pressure around my neck increases

And then it happens

All hell breaks loose

The rivers flow with an intensity

The power that he had not a clue

He screams my name and loses all

His grip tells me that his release has come

Regardless if he was ready or not

And as he was calming down

My name slowly slipped from his lips

All I heard was damn!

Submissive and power all at the same time

His intelligence captured me

Pushed me

Pulled me

Wrapped me

And lullabies me to sleep

From the moment go

And the words that kept me coming back for more

I needed to be stimulated

While my body was manipulated

Nipples sucked until they were harder than polished steel

And they wanted more

The lines of pain and pleasure

Crossing highways that carry from east to west and back

north to south

At a speed that keeps the pleasure coming

I release sounds that equate to a foreign language

As his lips continue to devastate in a good way

They deserted my nipples and found a swollen clit

That was lit

On fire

Begging for attention

Did I mention

That now my hands are locked in prison

As he has his way with what is now swollen

Waiting to explode

I tossed and turned and to no avail

I couldn't get loose

And to be honest I didn't want to

I wanted him to continue

Pleasure and pain

Pain and pleasure

Over and over again

My pussy begged and pleaded

Even when my mind exploded within

Suddenly he entered with a force that made my voice

Scream from true pleasure with a taste of sweet pain

Dick that reached my dreams

He gave me more than most receive in a lifetime

And I plan on keeping him in mine

If only I could taste and explore him

As he has me

To see

If I can make his fantasies

Come true…..

He never knew

Never thought what was

Or what could be

As he sat and watched me from a distance

The passion that boiled deep inside when I caught just a glance

And if he just happened to come close

His scents, made chills run the length of me

Wrap me in wanting and seal me in I gotta have

Yes, his scent beyond intoxicating

It gave me a sense of assurance that he possessed

Not me

But I did feel it

Or it just may be the desire to have him, scratch that

At this moment…..all I wanted was to ride the waves

Conquer that stallion and be at his beck and call

His eyes undressed me

As my yoni screamed Yes!

But that wasn't enough

I needed enough to satisfy last year's deficit and my future
gain

And he could handle that just with the work of his tongue

I wanted to feel the Fourth of July fireworks from the
inside not in the sky

When given the chance I would take it but not before

I wanted not needed

And there is a difference

The chase had to be all his

And I would eventually allow myself to get caught

Once caught I would pleasure him from the front door

To be bedroom floor

And that is just the appetizer

The bed will enjoy the main course as the shower

Will allow for the breaks that will be needed

To lick and suck in merry-go-round motion

He will become my morning, noon and evening devotion

And the flavors

Baskin Robbins needs to add 69 to the menu

As we believe in sharing the pleasure

My mind is racing

Body strung out on thoughts of what can

What will be

And dammit when

The chase is real

As I sit and wait……

Visual place of Ecstasy

He whispered could he?

I responded can you?

He didn't realize that at that very moment

My want had turned into need

My lust had flipped over into greed

And the talking was definitely un-necessary

Because …..

His words was not what I wanted to taste

His lies would not grace me

I wanted none of that

I held my finger to his lips and whispered in his ears

Please don't speak

I need your tongue to go to work

Sucking my breast

And licking the rest

I want your tongue to do a work out as if it was at the gym

Yes you will put in some reps

Your hands need to caress

Massage and manipulate all of me

Yes you figured it out

Baby this is long overdue

So let's get started

I want to be stroked by chocolate steel

With precision

Hitting all the right spots and some that I didn't know
existed

Please don't

Not yet

Right there

Dammit

The rhythm is funky jazz with a reggae beat

That keeps you on repeat

Giving it to me just the way I like

See no need for words when I have the skills of your lips

Without sound

And then I whisper

Stop

You look hurt

Surprised and ready to plead your case

And my eyes said it all

You stepped back just enough

And at that very moment

I tasted the fruits of your labor

And your eyes rolled snake eyes

I stopped long enough

To whisper

You tasted me now I plan on tasting your emotions

And I swallowed…..

Sensual Evolution

He slipped

Didn't realize the power that she possessed

Or he did and got caught again

See he thought he knew

And

He slipped

Avoided her all week

One word conversations over text

Made it through the week

And

He slipped

Needed to make a quick visit

In and out

And when he laid his eyes on her it was over

Honey glazed eyes with sunshine skin

Breast full that speak to you before anything else does

He touched them

And it was over

He slipped

He kissed her lips and touched the other ones

Her yoni was hot and wet

As he caressed her clit her moans escaped

He removed his finger and quickly inserted in between her
lips

She sucked his finger like a Popsicle and moans escaped
his lips

Before he could speak she was on her knees

Sucking his dick with a smile

Tasting his emotions with every swallow

By now it was too late to turn back as she whispered in his
ear

I want to ride you….please

She repeated and before she knew it he was undressing and
so was she

She climbed the mountain and rode down the other side

He squeezed her melons and the rivers dam broke

And all hell broke loose

He screamed her name again and again

She rode him so well

That when she finished he was at a loss for words

He did more than slip

He was so out done that he needed her to dress him

He was late to the meeting

But walked in with a smile

The power that she possesses

He slipped and when he got up

His whole world was changed never to be the same

again….

I want you to make love to my mind....

sex my body....

and fuck my fantasy until you become my reality.....

allowing the very thought of you to turn on the faucet of

nectar that runs....

deep...

the ability to see you....

and with no words spoken.....

steel arises....you....

walk through my door....

and all inhibitions....

drop...no rules....

no if and or buts....

just pure pleasure....

and as I rise....

the moment comes when my pussy comes sliding down the

rod of steel....

the rhythm kicks in....

and you get the ride of a lifetime....

allowing all of you to seek out the depth that resides in

me...

each stroke came with another need...

hard and strong hitting all the g-spots that exist....

some that I didn't know existed....

you pulled back and re-entered me with power....

that shook my thoughts....

rearranged my outcome of pleasure.....

the moments approached as the juices continued to stir...

and you licked and sucked my nipples...

one hand wrapped around my neck.....and then...

with the intentions...

of your ride and my pleasure exploding....

all at the same damn time....

make love to my mind....

and I will fuck you pass reality

Orgasmic Dance

She needed to reach that take me around the world orgasm

And he needed to release so hard that it may be heard
around the world

Her pussy wanted to milk him for all he was worth

While he was determined to tame her rivers

Words not needed

As he stood behind her with his arm around her waist

His fingers found a waiting heated pot that he slowly
dipped in

He paused to feel the heat engulf his finger as he
envisioned his tongue taking its place

He slowly removed it and slowly slid it in her mouth

As far as it would go

She moaned at the taste of herself

And then moaned again for more

Intoxicating as it was he needed more

And was intent on getting it

Clothes fell to the floor

Heat continued to rise

He bent her over and slowly started his tongue bath of her

Licking and sucking wherever his lips could

Harder and harder as his dick grew

He knew he was ready to fuck her into the vision of his
fantasy

Legs spread and his tongue dives in

Inserted as far as it would go

And then

In and out

Out and in

And suddenly she begs him to stop

Only for her to take him deep in a 69 position

So he quickly resumed his position

She sucked and he licked

He sucked and she licked

They continued until the first of many orgasms flowed

After a few

She begged to ride

He stretched out and she straddles the stallion

And went for the ride of a lifetime

And just as she was about to explode

His hands wrapped around her neck and squeezed just
enough

For the rivers to overflow

Her body went into convulsions

With continuous orgasms

And more and more

And he wouldn't let go until every drop of her

Released

She screamed

She spoke in more than one language as they kept coming

And when the last one came

He spoke

That was round one

Are you ready for the next?

Souljistic Trifecta

Stimulate my mind...

with the depths of you....

fuck my body...

with orgasms that overflow...

but for this to last...

you have to make love to my soul...

reaching as far as the sun rises over the moon...

and then sets on the ecstasy that lies between us...

mind body and soul...

without all three....

we shall remain incomplete.....

and this is my EROTICA....deep rivers

"Chameleon's Interlude"

Nobody has a clue or do they

The rush that fuels my flames

Intensifies my fire and craving that I must have

He is my addiction

As I am his

Submissive in every since of the word

And his eyes let me know that I am his drug

Submissive yes, but I hold the power in the palm of my
hand

His energy drained as my needs are strong

I feel each stroke and I want more

With each lick, I need his tongue to rendezvous with all of
me

Tasting every flavor that rests upon my flesh

As his flesh, wet and hot, drenched with the sweat of me

Pheromones that reached the top of the hill and cascade
down the other side

And yes I am his submissive, but he is my toy

Then darkness arrives and the flesh

All alone needing to be caressed

And your voice appears before you

And I close my eyes and venture into another hidden
surprise

The darkness that brought pure chocolate to my door

Yes he arrived and my fear stayed on the other side of that
closed

Door….

Yes stripped and devoured with no words spoken

Sweet chocolate with a swirl of honey to accompany it

He licked and I sucked and wrapped myself in pure
darkness

That I didn't want light to shine upon

Yes he fed me all the flavors that his body could sustain

And then the explosion happened

He dripped cream all over my honey and the flavor we created

Our own sweet Honey Do....

My appetite needed to be satisfied and yet I still

Need

Want

And desire

The flavor that only exists in my dreams

If only I could sleep in my fantasy until it becomes my

Reality

My here and now

The end to my beginning

The dam to the river that flows

But only in my dreams......

I swallowed his taste.....and inhaled his flavor.....wrapped his warmth....and fanned the heat...as his eyes...stripped my soul....while his lips drank of my spirit....and we have yet to meet....under the moonlit tree...but our souls....swim the across the sea....of one day....deep rivers

Chambered Adventures

The desires of the heart mind and soul.....escaped....lost in a mirage of emotion....my heart longs to be loved.....my mind needs to be stimulated....never isolated.....while making love to my soul.....stroke more than the heat...between my thighs....eye to eye.....stimulate all that I entail.....to forever have all that your heart mind and soul desire....locked with mine....deep rivers

Love's Footnote

I want you to love me now

Love me tomorrow

Love me when I forget to love myself

But most of all, allow me to love you......deep rivers

Ecstasy Anticipation

I need to feel him

I need him to feel me

But most of all I need to feel forever

The lasting strokes of eternity

Wet kisses that will allow the rivers to flow

Flow with a strength that the waves crash with intensity

My desire slips above and beneath the crevices of passion

My addiction to be fulfilled

A combination of pleasure and pain

That feeds more than the average craving

Going from 0-100 in seconds

As the building of what is to be

Gravitates beyond the sky

Through the atmosphere with winds that take you from wet
to tsunami

Rapidly gasping for breath

As he continues to stroke deep wide and often

And the words that escape at that moment

Don't stop

Please

Don't

Stop

Yes

More

And

More

Yes the request for more not less

The battle to control or be controlled by my addiction…..

Am I feeling all that is present

Does he feel me

Thoughts of him

Reliving the first words that touched

Reaching so far down in the pit of my soul

the essence of all things right or wrong

not knowing which but non the less wanting

to fly free as sky above

to taste

the sweetness of sweet mangoes

juice flowing

flowing quenching more than a thirst

but a need that has never ended

and needed to be fed

touch me

with a soft caress like the petals of an African violet

as my heart beats stronger than a African drum

I crave

what I have yet to find

or have I

so far

but so close

and still I crave...

"Honesty's Erotic Core"

I tossed and turned

And realized that without attending to my

Deepest craving

The sleep would never arrive at my address

His words bled deep into my wounds

Eyes that spoke to my soul

And I have yet to meet him

The one that can satisfy

I know that I want to taste

His flavor

Devour all that he is

I need him to

Lick

Suck

Taste

And stroke me into another world

His world

I want him to feel my emotions

Fuck me pass all the hurt and pain

And make my body come alive

His body and mine

Sharing juices that create a drink

To quench my thirst

Good until the last drop

And then I want more

To straddle you

Placing you deep in my sacred temple

That will send chills

Up my spine

Sweat that will pour down my back

While your hands squeeze

Melons

With nipples that require your utmost attention

Twisting and sucking them to ripeness

I need your heat

Your fierce demands

Sensuality is not for tonight

I need hardcore

Hair pulling

Ass slapping

Throat choking

Deep stroking

Making me beg for more sex

We can make love another time

My body wants to go into overdrive

As the cravings

Are more than one or two

I need it all

All that you can give

Over and over

Again

Again

And

Again

Make me beg for it

Drop to my knees

To swallow all of you

And then again

Yes you are my addiction

And I need a fix

Long and hard

I need you……my fix….

Destiny's Soul Search

He whispered.....I found my soul mate

and my thoughts were the same

I couldn't respond as my smile was in full bloom

The moment when all seems so right

or is it wrong

but feels right

I haven't determined that

I just know that at that moment

that second

in time

I felt like a butterfly

flying free

and high

above all

that once mattered

Realizing that life

is truly to be lived

enjoyed

discovering the intricate secrets

of someone

the one

one

who

made

you feel

more than alive

real

without the games

the deception

delusion

His words were real

concrete

the black rose

the bloomed in hard reality

he saw pass

all that and made me smile....

The Rebirth of Love's Orientation

I want to taste you beneath the rainbow of reality

Lick you tears before they decide to fall

My reality has turned into more than a lifetime movie

As of this

Very

Moment

The reality

I have fallen

For the reality of your dreams

Kiss me

So that

I

Know its

Real

You reached far inside

Of the spectrum that

Creates the dreams that I keep sealed

And you

Opened a cocoon that will soon be

Beautiful butterflies

Flying over the emotions

Of my soul

Give and you shall receive

Deceive

And

The tears will fall from your very own

Eyes

My love is that of that dreamer

Wanted more than most will

Ever

Ever

Receive

Strokes that come down strong and hard

But bring the softness of a beautiful flower

With the pouring rains

Of my

Orgasms

And

I request more

And

More

Fluttering

To the head

Of your

Imagery

Taste me

Absorb

My spirit

With yours

As we

Become one

Entity

Facing the world of destiny

With every word that spills to paper

My desires rise

I started with a fantasy

That slowly grew into a need

A want

The beast that lay dormant deep inside

To be released

His words opened the door

And the beast escaped

On the prowl

With an even stronger need

Want

Desire

Raw

Explicit

Fight to be explored

Bend my needs to fit

The heat of the sun

Hot animalistic bodies that grind hard

Strokes that come down with the beat of African drums

And the strength of steel

Ass slapping

Throat choking

Making you beg for more

Or throw in the towel if you can't handle

Never to give up

Only to request for more

Begging to be taken to the moon and back

Sweat everywhere with the taste of pure seduction

Yes

It has happened never to return

The beast that is on the prowl for her prey

Capturing your darkest secrets

The hidden pain

That brings about pleasure

More than the average can withstand

And then he screamed

Nut went everywhere

And she relished in it

By asking

Can we go again?

I want to lie next to you

With my head on your chest breathing in sync

As my mind screams in silence

The pleasure to feel you

Soft kisses placed on your chest

While my hands venture the length of you

Exploring all that you are

As my lips take turn tasting you

I want to take this very slow

With visions of what is to come next

One delicacy after the other

Sweet and full of flavor

Intoxicating myself on you

To have waited this long

And to be honest I would wait even longer to grace

Your

Presence

To

Lick you

Suck you

And

Fuck you

From your reality

Into

My fantasy

One step at a time

My heat rises

More and more

Juices start to stir

Fingers dip into a honey pot

And allow you to taste

What you

Have created

Yes that very moment when your eyes

Smile

I know from that moment

All my days will be filled

With pleasing you

Straddled for the ride of your life

"Willing Prisoner…..Unwilling Victim"

I opened up

Allowed him to slip in

Under my deepest dreams

Not just the surface

He went deep

His words rest upon my breast

As each letter slowly trickled down the length of me

Finding their way to my hidden treasure

I allowed him in

So I can't

Won't

Be

Even though

I want to

Be

Mad at him

See the reality is that his lips

Never touched mine

They took them captive

With each melody that he placed in my heart

Hopes and dreams

That

He laid out for the two of us

And in all actuality

He hit the switch so quick

That I never saw it coming

And refuse to believe

What my ears felt

I really don't know what to say

Or do

I just know

At this very

Moment

He holds my heart hostage

With no release in sight

When poetry deceived me

I lost the battle

So who will win the war?

The mind that never rest

the

music

plays

a different tune

than the sounds around me

trapped in the moment

of

reality

fighting to reach

fantasy

but

he

is

so damn

far away to touch

but I feel all that he is

I feel him more than he feels his self-Talented with gifts

that

shine

but can he walk on

the dark

side

of

where

I reside

sweat dripping

heat rising

with a tongue bath that misses not one

special

spot

hot from the stirring of what he fears

to dive deep

in rivers

that flow

giving life

beyond any that he has ever known

he whispers

and it is done

pleasure placed

from the top to the tip of his soul

yes words

started a fire

that will forever burn

the fantasy

that

has

now

become the reality that leaves him speechless

Deep rivers a continuous flow of ecstasy

Addiction's Unforgiving Rapture

At moments like this

my mind battles

with my soul

whispers to my spirit

as if whispering makes a difference

I shall only listen to the voice that

gives me

feeds me

fulfills me

demands attention

commands my body and mind in dimensions

that only the voice knows how far I can go

See I know the truth is so much better than a lie

I admitted to myself

a long

time ago

diagnosed

accepted

My addiction

fire

that never burns out

fanned by the flames

and it still is Hot in Here

I need nipples licked

sucked

and fucked

while my body responds

to hands that explore

deep spaces

hidden places

that you ace

when located

needing long strokes

fast then slow

while your lips continue to

assault what needs attention

you slowly place your hands and squeeze

dick in place

lips assault with grace

and the explosion of the deep valleys flows

yes I am an addict

and my only therapy is

Let's go another round.....

Erotically Written....Deep Rivers

Pursuit of Exclusivity

Slip into the den of misunderstanding

words that don't need

to be

explained

as you

know

exactly

the true

meaning of deception

delusion

within my own eyes

desire

that lives behind

the cornea

waiting

contemplating

the next

move

that needs to be made

heights to reach

in the clouds of

the impossible

and I still reach for all that is there

my instincts keen

and never blind

to what is before me

know and trust

the mind of a word master

reading between

behind

and over the words that spill so gracefully

to the pages

your cockiness

will have you miss the reward

that most never receive

tired

drained

as my mind never seems to rest

as greatness is just over the valley

and my eyes will not rest until it is mine

slip into the den of understanding

Conscious Fluidity

Inspiration that flows deep

into the valley

and then all over us

flowing like melted chocolate

ready to lick every drop

the reality is

hot

amazing

graphics

that create imagery

that makes juices stir

and nectar flow

waiting as he catches every drop

of who I am

words that speak volumes

with a mere whisper

eyes that speak to your soul

words that write the smooth ending to tragedy

and in the same breath

breathe life into what once was gone

inspiration that strips your of any hidden fears

power play

he is that and so much more....inspiration

His words walked through my thighs....

and spelled....

heat....

fire....

scrumptious nectar....

as I opened them wider....

so he could spell the outcome....

he desired the waterfall ....

and I watched as he tried to break the dam....

can he...

maybe....

will I allow him....

to....

give him the opportunity. ..

to enter my prize possession. ...

stimulate who I am....

see most forget that the greatest possession is the mind of

understanding....

stimulate my mind....

and I will fuck you into your future....

With me

You opened the door on the dark side

exposed the emotions that ride

deep inside

I am the deep valley

that flows with an infinity

of nectar

I am my sexuality

sensuality

and the beast that preys

for the heat

that erupts the rivers

of eternity

my tongue slowly gives

a bath of you

from head to base

tip to soul

licking

sucking

and swallowing all of you

as you scream more than my name

you realize

that the dark side

of pure passion

elevated with

the power that the beast

releases

you

moan

scream

beg for more

as my tongue

assaults

you

allowing you the pleasure

to enjoy

fucking you to the moon and back

and then with hands wrapped around my neck

dick stroking the merry go round

you squeeze just enough

for the waterfalls to erupt

to the heavens above

as you drink the sweetest nectar

your lips have ever had

and this will continue

as the beast has now

been

released

I placed you between my lips

Licking

sucking

tasting

pressured applied

just right

straddled

merry go round

slow

then fast

up then down

pussy muscles suck you in

and grip your dick

and just when you

moan

louder

and

then

scream

my name

my lips swallow you whole

to the back of my throat

and hold you right there

as my throat

muscles

milk all of you

and you beg

me

to

stop

but

your emotions I needed to taste

I didn't need a picture

The image embedded in my mind

on my lips

and deep in

my soul....

He touched me

where no one has ever

reached

or tasted

with hands of strength

or a tongue

of skill....

See he

licked me softly

sucked me gently

and then

restrained me

so that what he

decided to do next

all I could do is enjoy.....

from a loud slap

on my ass

to nipple clamps that sent

sensations

from the bottom of my feet to

the tips of 42 DD breast

that longed for more

He stood in from of me and teased me

with a dick that was hard as steel and wet and wanting

to enter deep.....

He stroked my lips with his dick

and then

forced his dick in my lips and hit the back of my throat

with precision

in and out

and then he stopped, walked around behind me and

with all the strength he had

he entered me.....deep

hard and long

he continued to stroke me

as screams and moans escaped my lips

the combination of pain and pleasure

had me begging for more.....

I needed no picture.....close your eyes

and you will visualize

the pleasure

I received.....

That moment when you need

to be kissed

licked

sucked

fucked

and then start all over again

I want your tongue

to paint a masterpiece

and my body is your canvas

take your hands and explore

touch

squeeze

suck

and stroke

all of me

touch my clit

so that you feel

the heat

sensitive

but waiting for your lips

to visit

i want to be stimulated

my mind first

body second

soul third

and then

when all

is done

I want to squirt all over you

again and again

feel the juices that release

tasting a nectar

sweeter than honey with a juice flow of sweet mangoes

I want to play with you

touch you

taste you

and stroke your dick until you beg me

to enter my pussy with a stroke of true precision

hitting all the g-spots you can find

and then you can fuck me into your reality.....

The Love Letter....By Deep Rivers

You sent me a letter that quite frankly swelled the tears in

my eyes and the lump in my throat

see for me love has always came hard

I love hard and always pay the price with my emotions

splattered again

So as I read you words

I ponder can it be, is it possible for one to really love

Me

to feel the love

that I give from deep within

never to walk away,

my love will die for his

I give until the well runs dry

so I ask myself does he feel my love

To share a friendship

that battles between our beliefs

as we will agree to disagree

to understand that

I love you mean

s I am not alone and neither are you

To feel my heat rise

my words whispered

that land on your lips

swallowed in the pit of your soul

simple but complex words

meaning the protection of my heart

See

I slowly watched my eyes fall in love

with you

my heart get encased in your hands

as my hope to love again

for infinity

not the moment

I knew when I said the words out loud

You would hear me whisper

I Love You.

Or did you hear at all situations

That complicate what can be only if we let them

I see you in my dreams that bring me heat

Causing my breathing to go astray

Wanting you to take me

I almost believed what was not real

I knew then that my broken heart needed

To be healed so that the love that came for

A lifetime stay

can stay with

She wants more than the physical One

A quest to obtain the physical with

The spiritual love that which goes deep

For the two

She believes as her soul comes back

To life with the kiss of his spirit they are love...

"Erogeneous Winds of Euphoria"

The storm is full blown

The music plays a melody

That only are souls take in

Feel

Breathe in

Bodies stir with intensity

To clear the dance floor

As those that watch

Take notes

Your eyes

Dictate all that my body does

Your touch heats

More than my soul

It gives life to mine

Bringing my soul alive

You escape into my deepest dreams

Walking through my fantasies

And complete the orgasms

To explosion

Watering the flowers that bloom

In the darkest of night

But with a kiss of light

As the valley flourishes

With your words

The light in your eyes

Know that nothing else

Can be

What I deliver

The aroma that entices the room

Dressed in the colors

That bring passion

To what we have

The darkness to light

Is what we are.....

I wanted him to kiss me

Deep with tenacity to feel my innermost thoughts

Whispering what you are planning to do with and to me

Your lips slipped to my ear round the back of my neck

And then

I first something cool on my neck

As you blew on my neck chills ran the length of my spine

You whispered, I will lick your clit the same

Chills continued

With one arm around my waist

You slowly stripped me not allowing me to move

Control was totally not mine

I begged to be released

And you asked why

I couldn't give a good enough answer so you continued on
your mission

My hands were quickly tied

And my body placed on the bed

Before I knew it

Legs spread eagle and restrained

Damn

Was all I could say

Now this wasn't the first time

But the look in your eyes said it would be different

Than before

I felt cold then hot

I felt hands that explored and it was more than just yours

My eyes could not see as you had blindfolded me as well

No voices, just hands and then lips

Your lips reconnected with mine but someone else's lips
were sucking on my clit

Damn it felt amazing

At this point I didn't care

I needed to be taken to the highest heights and brought to
multiple orgasms

You dick found my lips and I began to feast on you

My pleasure became yours

While I was being licked

Sucked

And eventually fucked

I licked

Sucked

And eventually swallowed you

Allowing your dick to hit the back of my throat

And held you there

As I felt the heat rising

I knew it was time

I sucked you in deep once more and we both

Exploded at the same damn time

Sweet pleasure even better

When you removed the blindfold it was just you and I

No questions asked…..

Fantasy's Boast…..Reality's Glow

He slowly removed the blinders from my words....

placed his lips upon my treasure....

devoured the delicacy of me....

hands that traveled the valley...

in search of hidden intimacies....

my words found their voice....

as I whispered the emotions that hide....

take me....

stroke me..

Lick me….

Taste the depth of the beast….

As the momentum builds....

The strength of you yields...

I am more than you will ever know….

My hidden addiction…..

That craves many stimulants….

attention directed to all that is affected....

by the strokes of precision....

that create a rhythm....

that sing a melody....

with the touch of bass....

my words speak louder and louder...

as the strokes get stronger and stronger....

as the storm erupts...and the explosion is never ending....

you removed the blinders of my words...so the expression
could flow....

as you satisfied more than my soul….

You reached deep….

My spirit experienced an awakening….

While the mental battled at what was ….

What will be….

Or can be….

I want to be set free…..

As my desires is more than just fantasy….

They are reality…..

"Emotional Clairvoyance"

The depth of my inner mind....runs away at times with thoughts...that give me many words....many emotions...the ability to see....what is not there....to taste the flavor....that I go in search.....that searches for me.....to experience love and warmth.....that caresses....strokes the curve of my face.....holds the imperfections that are perfect at the right time....I am the epitome of love...the desire of want.....and the capability of need....see as the moon glows over the sun in my eyes....that bleeds understanding....a heart of now....deep rivers

He slow walked his tongue through my dreams

As his words played melodies upon my breasts

I knew has each word released from his lips

That I patiently waited for them to land upon my lips

And he would lick them so that I knew he was present

I need to feel him

deep

in

my

soul

and his words did just that

They careful licked

sucked

and fucked me from my fantasy

into his reality

and

I

waited

patiently

as his words formed

to escape once more to my lips

hungry for his knowledge

thirsty for his intelligence

and addicted to his

dick

yes I wanted it all..

My pussy decided that she had demands

Demands that I couldn't keep up with

The late night cravings

Early morning lust

Midday got to have it

and what was I to do

Trying to stay on the side of caution

And all she wanted was the next thrill

Hard strokes that would be given

At the drop of whistle

She wanted to be licked

Sucked

Fucked

and sucked some more

to be caressed

slapped

and choked

before the rivers would flow

and then

to have it over and over again

posted up like boot camp

she demanded to be pleased

to feel your dick

deep inside

hitting the bottom of all that she was

addicted to what gave her chills up and down her spine

thrills that made her taste you on her lips

long after you were gone

She wanted what we needed

Desired what most couldn't give her

And yet you thought she was mistaken

that what you gave was more than sufficient

She is insatiable

hungry

to be fed

so stroke her

taste her

lick and suck the life

and then allow her to breath for more...

Part 2

He said he wanted more

Took in a long breath and wanted more

so I obliged

I straddled him and just sat there

looked deep into his eyes

and said let's go for a ride

the ride of a lifetime

first to experience a merry-go-round

slow then fast and just right

see I wanted to hear him moan my name

scream what he wanted me to do

As I slowly spun around

on a dick that was bringing me much pleasure

and rode him as I heard his moans even more

I stopped

un mounted him

and resumed the pleasure

with my lips wrapped around him

I licked from the head to the base

and back down

My tongue did tricks with the head of his dick

that made him need to breathe again

and I let him

I wanted him to enjoy every step

to show him my gratitude for the satisfaction

that he gave to me

so I went back in

I sucked his dick

better than any lollipop I ever sucked as child

He possessed a flavor that I had to have

chocolate

filled with creme

My pussy throbbed with each taste

and then the ultimate

I took his dick deep between my lips

and swallowed

as his dick hit the back of my throat

I continued to swallow

and enjoy the screams of passion

that he released

and just when he was about to release

I stopped

straddled him

and fucked him into my reality

up to this point it had just been a fantasy

that will forever make him smile.....

My days and nights

The in between hours that flutter

About in the midst of the wicked

While being a wounded butterfly

When loves hides and last replaces

In the chair reigning supreme

Heat beyond the fire

Of gesture

But the righteous heir to a thrown

That gives only to wait

To receive

Tasting

Licking

Fondling

Caressing

Stimulation

That runs from the outside in

Needing to be taken to heights that

Only addiction knows

The true definition of her desires

She slips into a mirage of how deep

He should go and deep is never

Deep enough

She craves for more each time he

Completes the task of the insatiable appetite

That lays before him

Exhausted and she wants more

To continuously feel him penetrating

To the core of her lava

She is addicting to the sensations

That run from her toes through the eyes of knowing she

wants more

She loves to explodes over and over

Again

Then to explode even more

An emotion that brings the fullness that her soul desires

Orgasms after orgasms

Moans of beauty

When he whispers my name

As he is exhausted with no air left to scream

She wishes for more than the normal

She needs to feel needed

Wanted and desired

That his thoughts start and end

With her lips pressed to his

Exploring the flavor of sweet honey

To know his arms caress and protect at the same time

That they will stroke her deeper than before

Giving her all that her desires

While satisfying the heat that rises between her thighs

She is his fantasy

Turned reality

With continuous licks from her tongue

With lips that swallow the length of him

Allowing him to breath and then swallow again

She wants to sit at his feet and listen to his mind

The straddle him once again to see how his mind works

Behind closed doors

She is his escape

As he is her knight

They are together the power that never ceases

As they go higher than the last dream

And this is their reality

Multiple orgasms with multiple ways to achieve them....

Erotically Penned by Deep Rivers

"Anticipation of Waiting"

His hands were the brushstrokes of my soul.....

delicate strokes that tiptoe through my tulips.....,

while my soul stirred with the capability of what is....

he doesn't know....

doesn't feel the rush....

of the sunlight that reaches out across the sea of

contemplation....

in the meantime a heart waits for adoration.....

cultivation of mental thoughts....

that supersedes all understanding....

he is...

will be....

while wet kisses......

that have yet to be received....

bring a smile to a heart that is waiting.....

I closed my eyes and your words

Drifted deep inside of me

Yes as I pulled on thigh high knee socks

My hands continued up the path to your destiny

And my sanity

I needed you to slowly enter

And then play beautiful music

But only for a moment

I have no reason to lie

I want more than music

I need hardcore

Stripping

Savage

Lovemaking

Scratch that

I need you to fuck me into your reality

Give me the best of all of you

A tongue that licks me like fresh scooped ice cream

Hands that assault my body with pleasure

And strokes from hard steel

That goes all night long

No time for intermission

I needed

Crave it

Desire

And damn well deserve

Put your lips on my lips

And cause my heat to rise

Spilling my life onto your attention

And tasting all of your worldly possessions

Slide down my throat

Like smooth silk

And we knew that this was the start

As you grabbed my hair

And pulled hard

And whispered

Can you take

All that I have to give

So I whispered back

Give me all that you can

And more

I need it

I want to feel the strength of you

Deep

Deep

Then deeper

And only then will I tell you

How much more I really want

Really need

As you continue to feed my addiction.....you…..

My eyes deceived me

While my thoughts ran away with my deepest thoughts

Taking what they wanted

As the shy

Hidden

Timid

Loving

Side of me stood by and watched

An out of body experience

That can only be explained by the juices that flowed

From between my thighs

His voice

Commanded

Demanded

And sweet talked me into the beast

Within

Deep inside that once released

Takes complete control

Shutting out any reasoning that hails from the side of sanity

My breathing swelled

Chest beating faster and faster

And I had lost or given up all control

Rational thoughts went out the damn window

And the chills

The cold sweats

The explosion that rang out in my mind

Body and soul

And then I realized

My addiction was in full control

Once again

My cravings

Desire

Wants

Needs

And sweet nothings

Had no answers

But one

I walked through sub drop

And was all alone

To want again

Once upon a time

Only in my mind

There is no once upon a time in my head

All that exists

Is wants

Needs

And tears

That never ceases to appear

Without the reality of what is

And then a pen

Crossed

My many thoughts

Punctuating my dreams

And hyphenating

My reality

The ink bled in many colors

Of hope

Peace

And love from the depths of an ink well

That never runs dry

The possibilities are infinite

The battle that

Will right

Or write

Its own ending

Or maybe not

But the path shall not

Go without the caresses of my pen

The seduction

Of whom I am

And all that hibernates

Deep

Will rise and dance with…..sensational lines

I sit by the water and think quietly

the water has become the music to my words

a rhythm that comes crashing down

upon bare breasts

cleansing me of nothing

giving me yet another reason to write

I know he has no clue

all this time

moments stolen to gaze in his eyes

and then smile

thoughts of what I want to do

so I close my eyes

straddle him

take him deep inside

and sit very still

he is blindfolded

I take his hands and let them explore

touching and feeling

with my direction

my hand on top of his

guiding them and allowing them to squeeze

melons as that invite him

nipples hard

wanting to be fondled

twisted

pulled

pain and pleasure

you know what I like

and then I stop you

hold your hands

and slowly go in circles while you are still

deep inside

I listen for the moans

that are now escaping your lips

and the speed increases

and then slows

but stays steady

and then fast

then slow

the moans

replaced by explicit words

that are music to my ears

as you beg me not to stop

and I don't know

if

you

have

realized

that I am more submissive

that you knew

I place your hands around my neck

and the speed

increases

and

now

the

moans are competing against

each other

and

then

I scream

tighter

and

you hesitate

and

I scream

tighter

again

this time you tighten

just a bit

and

then

a bit

more

you looked

deep in my eyes

and I closed mine

and released

the rivers flowed

which caused you to explode

and this happens every time

I close my eyes and think deeply of you

I looked into his eyes

The warmth that read through me

Was the switch that controlled the heat

Between my thighs

I needed to feel more than his touch

His lips were needed to

His hands were being summoned to

And his dick to follow the process that was in the making

My lips wanted to taste him at the same time

He tasted me

The look that I saw in his eyes

Stirred more than heat

It reached the mental stimulation

Creating a connection between two souls

Common sex not wanted

But what was needed

Was the depth of two souls to become one

As minds meet beneath the moon and stars

Twisted into what was that is no longer

Two souls that melt into the spirit of one

The give and take

He gives she takes

She rides and he receives

Nectar with cream

Sweeter than any flavor

From strokes that are stronger than steel

He continues until she screams more than his name

She drains every drop of cream that he can give her

And they breathe in sync

With the ability to hear

The power that is insatiable

Unlike any other

Unique as their D.N.A

They are

The sensuous sexual creatures of understanding

And not a word needed to be spoken

The reality of a façade is more than a storm at midnight

Seeing the trees for the forest

And getting wet all the same

Can you feel the connection of two souls?

Pulling in the same direction

Wanting to taste the flavor

Of emotions that spill to the pages

As the suns attempts to shine through raindrops

But the wind spins them into destiny

He feels hers lips play a melody up and down

The length of his steel

While his hands caress the melons that accentuates her

curves

She feels the vibrations with each touch

The heat from his hands is more than the sun

Upon her face

All a while the raindrops fall

Never cooling off the heat that has taken over her

Slowly they both undress

Each other

And lips continue on a journey of what pleasures them the
most

He listens has her breathing increases

As his hand finds her nectar

That spills for him

He clutches her

She wraps her fingers around him

And they both stroke each other to the rhythm of the
raindrops

As the sun peeks through to be the spotlight

Of their show

Better than Broadway

As they continue

Building each other to the explosion of a lifetime

The moans escape

From the two of them

As the moment has arrived

They both release

With screams of ecstasy

He is her

And she is him

At the moment they both give

And receive at the same time

Raindrops the back drops to the pleasure

That has started and they will continue

The moment in time

That created a connection between two souls

Never to be duplicated

As they are now one

That moment when the house is pitch black

and you smell his scent

your heart starts pumping

the heat between your thighs

kicks into high gear

you know what you want

and you know he is that one to give it to you

the pleasure that goes deep and dark

you strip as you head up the stairs

you goes straight for the shower

water hot

and you even hotter

fresh from the shower

you find your way

his scent get stronger

the closer you get to him

you reach

and he throws you on the bed

he caresses you from head to toe

lips find your breast

and the assault is pain and pleasure

he ties you down

and you know this means all night power play

he continues to suck

and lick your clit

soft then hard

his tongue goes deep

your moans get louder

and he never says a word

he fucks you hard and long with a tongue that won't quit

and just when your rivers start to flow

he mounts you

grips them hips

and rides the waves

straight from start to finish

he continues

you scream

and he fucks you harder

you have multiple orgasms

and he continues to fuck you

hitting every g-spot you have

and right before he comes

his dick slides between your lips

feeling the heat of your tongue

he fucks your mouth

and releases the strongest orgasm

you have ever felt

and then you realize

that he held back to just the right moment

to release

Dear Love,

If I wrote a love letter....

where would I start...

would it be complex....

or would it be simple....

I decided the complex simple way....

I love you....

deep rivers

Trashed emotions….

Words raped

As my pens ink dried

Illogical thoughts

That gives reason to pause

And then do it all over again

I need to feel again

His touch that sends more than a chill

It gives moments of absolution

Never an intrusion

My words

Are who I am

Not who you think they may be

See I close my eyes and let loose on reality

My mind goes faster at times

Than my finger can type

The juices stir

The heat on fire

And I become wet

With closed eyes that visualize you

Entering my voice that speaks

With strokes

Licks

Sucks

And hard fucking

My mind sees

And my lips feel

Hard flesh with a flavor that gives

Me more than a rush

Determination to drain you to fuel me

See I am that submissive that pleases until you scream my

name

And you allow me to continue

To bring you back to attention

Only to fuck you again

I want it all

Every last drop of intuition

That knows you need to feed my addiction

Give me more

Allow me to explode

Breathe

And then

I will fuck you over and over

Again

My desires never cease

They only aim to please

Forever

Walked in the door with only one thing on my mind

Washing off a long day

Soaking in a hot lavender bath

Taking my mind to a place of peace

Tranquility in my own sanctuary

Wrapped in warmth of subtle moments

As the heat of the water trickles down my back

With sensations that twist the inner juices

That sends messages that need to be addressed

But for this moment I bask in the lust of me

Hands that caress breast that allows nipples to stand

At full attention to what comes next

Twisting and squeezing my nipples as

They send jolts of yes

To sensuous places all through my body

I want to take this slow

Enjoy every touch

Ever you taste

Every lick

That I can give me

My eyes wide shut

As my ears see what the naked eye

Wishes for

See to explore one's self

Allows the mind to direct someone else

In the true art of pleasuring you

My hands find what has been patiently waiting

Your arrival

Caressing from the outside in

Finding that one place that needs to be stimulated

Going in circles

Squeezing and pulling the pleasure out

Of

As the excitement builds

Then I stop as I hear the door

Body waiting and willing

I want you to take me from my fantasy

To your reality

You enter and take me from one to the other

And start from the bottom and work your tongue

All the way to my treasure

Where my hands once were

Your tongue is now the master

My body twist and turns as your tongue goes deep

As I can only imagine what comes next

I see no longer as I have been blindfolded

Hands tied to each bedpost

And you whisper that you will have your way

Licking

Sucking

Probing

And fucking

Every part of me

As you continue to bring my body

To continuous orgasms over and over again

Erotic evades me

Sensual walked away

and the heat continues to rise

See the present moment of ecstasy

needs to licked

sucked

chocked

spanked

caressed

twisted

and manipulated

and then

and only then

can the ultimate take place

I need to be fucked

hard strokes

long continuous strokes

while you hit every g spot that exists

give me what my body

craves

deserves from head to toe

you can save the romance

for another time

the present time I need to feel the strength of your dick

deep

wide

and often

lips

wet

long

and willing

my pussy flows with the strength of your strokes

I am your submissive

and your wish is my command

He asked did I have a fetish

What turned me on

I asked why

Would he oblige

Or just ask to be asking

He responded

Baby the only way a man can please a woman

is to know what makes her tick

which way he should lick

her

How to stimulate her mind first

Caress her spirit

and the body will follow

but you must know what to do with it when it does

so obliged him

caress my breast

lick them

then suck

soft then hard

make them your own

he took mental notes

but he asked more

so I told him

after paying attention to my weak spot

you will know exactly where to place your lips

how to insert your dick

and at the same time

know when and where to place your hands

listening closely

will get the rivers to flow

the juices of sweet honey and mango

to satisfy your addiction for sweets

you listen

and your notes

will write the book....

Word Erotic Orgasms

His eyes burned deep into my soul

His lips played a melody with a body that craved

While his hands were the guitar strings that

Hit every note that I had in me

He whispered what he wanted to do

One step at a time

As his lips slowly explored

From my ear to the back of my neck

Down to the cleavage that awaited him

Attention paid to each breast

Nipples hard as diamonds

As he wet tongue teased and tortured each one

Moans escaped

Pleas of continuance

And he would whisper

No need to rush

I needed to have him

Feel him deep inside

But not before he took my mind

To a place that I didn't want to return from

My addiction needed to be fed

My pussy needed to be licked

Stroked

And explored in many ways

While my clit was given the ultimate stimulation

He knew exactly what I needed

Even what I wanted

And he gave me that and more

He gave details of all that he would do

And he did just that

As my pussy came over

And over

He continued to suck various places

And the rivers continued to flow

Juices that was sweeter than honey

He pleasured more than my body

My mind was given more than stimulation

He gives me knowledge of self

Loving so much more

As the flow goes both ways

I fucked him many ways

I needed to taste him to quench my thirst of him

To fill my emptiness

Yes he gave me dick of strength

As my lips swallow all of him

And then

We go again

Never ending pleasure

The fire that never burns out

desire that forever grows

in the pit of reality

as you know

his words

his tongue

his dick

and the most important

his mind

continues to manipulate

your body

your heart

your yoni

and the most important

your mind

to do things

that

you

and

others only dream about

he stimulates your mind

teaching and you hold on to his every word

his lips play musical chairs with the heat of you

while his hands

play dominoes

with your pussy

he sets each piece in place

and then gives that one powerful stroke

and the dominoes fall

in perfect form

as your body releases each orgasm

after orgasm

after orgasm

you scream for more

and whisper stop at the same damn time

and he does both

he stops deep embedded in your soul

the pulls back and slams into your reality

with hands placed around your neck just right

and the rivers break

the waters flow

from the depth of

deep rivers

Slip into the essence of passion

Ride the waves of seduction

With power strokes

Strong lips

And hands of strength

Take your tongue on a journey of ecstasy

Fresh mango juices flowing

To quench your thirst

Ride the rivers

Of deep waters

Penetrating my soul

Fucking me into a trance of pleasure

Begging for more

Hard dick meeting wet yoni

Slide Deep

And deeper

Caressing the G spots within

I need to feel every inch of you

In between my lips

Tasting the strength of your manhood

As with each stroke

You fuck me Into another time zone

Moans turn into screams of wanting more

Breathing harder with the intensity of you

Fuck me until the world comes to an end

And our explosion gives it back

Life

Erotically Penned by Deep Rivers

Spill

The very ink the spills from the cleavage of my dreams

See you have to possess eyes that see the darkness of my
desire

I am more than the rivers that

Spill

Flavors of Mangoes

Honey and sweet Papaya

Drenched in juices that flow with authority

I crave the reality

More

Lust

Hunger

Begging for lips to wrap steel and

Slowly Suck the Soul from you

I am the beast that has been released

My Prey awaits

Wet Nipples Hard as Bullets

Needing to be Sucked

an Insatiable appetite

explore all that is in sight

I am and will satisfy my hunger

as my lips take you deep

deeper in my sanctuary of hunger

A body that craves it all

I am the flow of deep rivers enter at your own risk....deep
rivers

I want to thank my readers that enjoy the erotic thoughts that flow from my mind body and soul. I have truly enjoyed each piece that has been written.

Thank you Jaimes Monroe, my brother in law that carefully placed titles to pieces in this book that are so fitting that I couldn't have created better ones myself.

You can contact me on facebook on my fan page

deep rivers

my email address is

deeprivers67@yahoo.com

Or you can listen in to my radio show

Red Cup Chronicles featuring Fix it Friday

with my beautiful co-host

the island gurl

every Friday from 7 pm – 9 pm

www.nuubeatradio.com

itunes

nuubeatradio

playstore

nuubeatradio